Everything Under The Sun For My Son

Cole Saini

This Book Belongs To

In the cradle of dawn's gentle light,

A father dreams with all his might,

Of worlds uncharted, yet to be spun,

For his beloved, his precious son.

"Everything under the sun," we'll say,

As we embark on witnessing the grand display.

Through meadows green and mountains high,

Underneath the endless sky.

We'll chase the whispers of the breeze,

And dance among the rustling trees,

With each step, a new adventure begun,

For this journey's just for father and son.

We'll marvel at the ocean's might,

As waves caress the shores so bright,

And count the stars, one by one,

As night unveils its kingdom my son.

In deserts vast where dunes reside,

We'll ride the winds, a daring glide,

Discovering secrets in the sand,

Together, the adventures will be grand.

In bustling cities, full of life,

We'll witness joy and sometimes strife,

Discover cultures, rich and bright,

And share the warmth of life's delights.

In forests deep, where shadows play,

We'll find new paths and light the way,

With every rustle, chirp, and hum,

A symphony of life's beat to the drum.

Through valleys deep and canyons wide,

We'll journey side by side,

With every wonder, every run,

In this world, everything under the sun.

In fields of flowers, we'll lose track of time,

While listening to nature's sweetest chime,

And learn from every setting sun,

That life's greatest treasures are shared, not won.

For a father's heart, forever spun,

With dreams of showing his precious one,

The beauty of this world, where all is won,

Underneath the golden, radiant sun.

About the Author:

Cole Saini is a devoted father and passionate storyteller who draws inspiration from the everyday moments shared with his family. The birth of his son sparked a deep desire to create stories that capture the wonder and beauty of the world. He lives with his wife and son in Manteca, CA, where they enjoy exploring the great outdoors and discovering new adventures together.

www.ingramcontent.com/pod-product-compliance
Lightning Source LLC
LaVergne TN
LVHW072348060726
842759LV00024B/122